What Animal Is That?

Indigo Lila's Whimsical World
Tales of a Tiny Trailblazer

Written by

Kimyatta N. Chaney

Copyright © 2024 Kimyatta N. Chaney
All rights reserved
First Edition

NEWMAN SPRINGS PUBLISHING
320 Broad Street
Red Bank, NJ 07701

First originally published by Newman Springs Publishing 2024

ISBN 979-8-89308-263-0 (Paperback)
ISBN 979-8-89308-268-5 (Hardcover)
ISBN 979-8-89308-264-7 (Digital)

Printed in the United States of America

Illustrated by:
Rafael Faustino Junior

To my loving granddaughter, Indigo Lila Chaney.
With all my love, Meemom ♡

This book is dedicated with all my love to my cherished granddaughter, Indigo Lila Chaney—your, inquisitive nature, joy, and spirit inspire every word. Special thanks goes to my sons, Vaughn and Jaidyn Chaney, for their unwavering love and support throughout this journey. A heartfelt thank you to my sister, my best friend, Tinika Chaney, who listened, read, and shared valuable insights at any hour, making this book a collaborative labor of love. Gratitude also extends to my dear friend of over thirty-five years, Michelle Lambert, for her consistent, honest, and supportive feedback that has enriched this creative endeavor.

With love,
Kimyatta N. Chaney

In a cozy home where laughter and love reside lives Indigo Lila, a spirited toddler with a heart as wild and free as her imagination. This is the delightful tale of a little explorer who always asks, "What animal is that?"

Every morning, Indigo's curious eyes would light up as she peered out the window, spotting creatures in the backyard. "Meemom, what animal is that?" she'd ask, setting the stage for a day filled with adventure.

Meemom, with a smile as warm as the sun, would join Indigo on their daily safari. Each day, a new discovery awaited—from imaginary lions in the bushes to colorful birds with songs that echoed through the air

With the memory skills of an elephant, Indigo soaked in every detail. She'd mimic the roar of a lion (*Roooaaar!*), the trumpet of an elephant (*Brrraaaahhh!*), and the chatter of mischievous monkeys (*Oo-oo-ah-ah!*), leaving Meemom in stitches with her playful mimicry.

Back indoors, the living room transformed into a jungle of pillows and blankets. Indigo, armed with her stuffed elephant, Arrow, led expeditions to uncover hidden treasures and meet imaginary friends in the depths of the sofa.

Mealtime became a feast of animal-shaped delights, with spaghetti serpents and pancake pandas. Indigo's giggles echoed as Meemom played along, turning ordinary meals into extraordinary moments of joy.

In the evening, bath time turned into a water safari. Bubbles became schools of fish, and rubber ducks transformed into majestic swans. "Meemom, look! What animal is that?" Indigo would exclaim, turning every splash into a new discovery.

As the moon lit up the night sky, Indigo snuggled into her favorite blanket, ready for bedtime tales. "Meemom, what animal will we meet in our dreams tonight?" she'd ask, closing the day with anticipation for tomorrow's safari of surprises.

The next morning, Indigo's excitement bubbled as she peered out the window. "Meemom, look! What animal is that?" She pointed to a flurry of colorful butterflies dancing in the sunshine.

9

With a twinkle in her eye, Meemom joined the adventure. "Those are the magical butterflies, Indigo. They bring joy to the world with their colorful dance." Indigo giggled, attempting to mimic the delicate dance of the butterflies.

Their safari continued to the backyard, where a chattering squirrel caught Indigo's attention. "Meemom, what animal is that?" she asked, eyes wide with curiosity.

11

Meemom chuckled, "That's a busy little chatterbox called Squeaky. He loves to tell stories to the trees and flowers." Indigo listened intently, trying her best to imitate Squeaky's lively chatter (*Chit chit chit*).

As they wandered, a gentle breeze carried the melody of birdsong. "Meemom, what animal is that?" Indigo pointed to a vibrant red cardinal perched on a branch.

Meemom smiled. "That's a musical maestro named Melody. She sings to the world and fills the air with joyous tunes." Indigo hummed along, creating her own sweet melody (*Mmmm hmmm hmmm hmmm hmmmmm*).

Back indoors, the living-room jungle awaited. This time, Indigo's sharp eyes spotted a fluffy, purring friend. "Meemom, what animal is that?" she asked, pointing to two snuggly cats curled up on the couch.

Meemom chuckled, "Aren't they purrfect! Our cozy companions Lucas and Harley. They love naptime and enjoy cuddling with us." Indigo mimicked purrs, creating a symphony of warmth and comfort (*Purr purr*).

At mealtime, a plate of spaghetti serpents slithered onto the table. Indigo giggled, "Meemom, what animal is that?" she asked, twirling her fork around the playful pasta.

Meemom grinned. "Those are silly serpents, Indigo. They're here to add a twist of fun to our meal." Laughter echoed as they enjoyed the whimsical feast together.

Bath time brought another splash of surprises.
"Meemom, look! What animal is that?" Indigo pointed
to a group of foam frogs hopping in the bubbly pond.

Meemom laughed, "Those are frothy frogs, Indigo. They hop and jump, bringing bubbly joy to our safari adventures." Indigo joined the imaginary pond, leaping alongside the frothy frogs.

Under the moonlit sky, Indigo snuggled into her cozy blanket, ready for bedtime tales. "Meemom, what animal will we meet in our dreams tonight?" she whispered, eyes shining with anticipation.

Meemom painted a dreamy picture of a celestial giraffe with star-spangled spots and a moonlit mane. "That's Stardust, the dream guardian. She watches over us and fills our dreams with magical adventures."

The night embraced them with sweet dreams and gentle slumber. In the morning, Indigo's eyes sparkled with a new question, "Meemom, what animal is that?" Their safari of surprises continued, a never-ending adventure of laughter and love.

A colorful parade of butterflies, chattering squirrels, melodious cardinals, and cozy cats filled their days. Silly serpents and frothy frogs joined the mealtime festivities, making every day a joyful celebration.

With each discovery, Indigo's laughter echoed through their cozy home, turning ordinary moments into extraordinary memories. Meemom cherished these precious days, where the wild heart of a little explorer transformed their world into a safari of surprises.

As they snuggled into bedtime tales, Indigo's heart swelled with gratitude. "Meemom, you make every day magical. What animal will we meet tomorrow?" she wondered, eyes filled with dreams.

Meemom smiled. "Tomorrow holds a new chapter of our safari, my little explorer. We'll discover creatures big and small, real and imaginary. But one thing is certain: it will be filled with love and laughter."

HOME Sweet HOME

And so the delightful tale of Indigo's Safari of Surprises continued, a heartwarming journey through the imagination of a spirited toddler and the endless wonders of the world around them.

As the sun dipped below the horizon, painting the sky with hues of pink and orange, Indigo whispered her final question, "Meemom, what animal is that?" The answer, she knew, was a canvas waiting to be painted with the vibrant colors of their tomorrow.

And as the moon lit up the night sky, Indigo drifted into dreams, her heart filled with the magic of a safari that would never end. In the arms of love, surrounded by the warmth of shared tales, she slept, ready for the countless adventures awaiting her.

This book, a treasure of shared moments and laughter, is dedicated to every little explorer and the grown-ups who join them on their safari of surprises. May your days be filled with wonder, curiosity, and the joy of asking, "What animal is that?"

About the Author

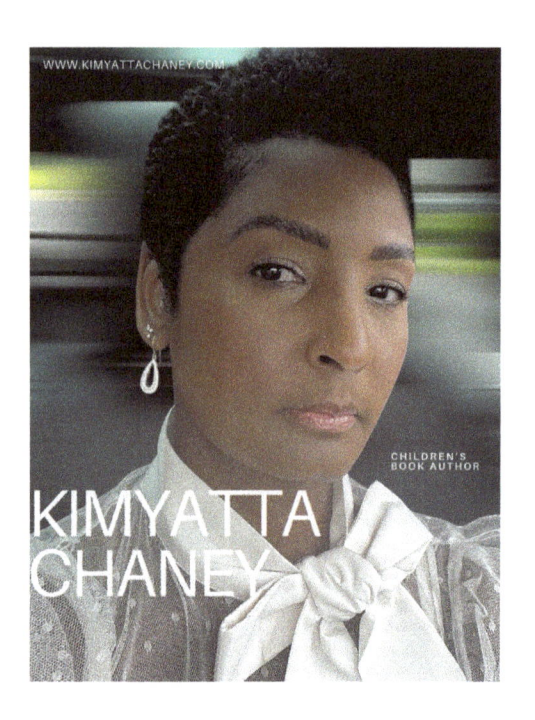

The author, a retired police officer of twenty-four years, is now venturing into children's literature with her debut work, *What Animal Is That?* Inspired by her granddaughter, Indigo Lila Chaney, the series, *Indigo Lila's Whimsical World: Tales of a Tiny Trailblazer*, captures her whimsical escapades. Each story promises warmth, love, and thrilling journeys. Beyond law enforcement, the author brings versatility with experiences in acting and business ownership. Join her on this heartwarming journey of togetherness and discovery.

Website: www.kimyattachaney.com